The
Cliff Birds
A Story of Hope

Written and illustrated by
Miles A. Moody

Recovery Communications, Inc.
P.O. Box 19910 • Baltimore, Maryland 21211 • (410) 243-4558

To receive our free monthly e-mail newsletter, please visit our website at
http://www.RecoveryCommunications.com

Dedication

To my wife, Lynne.

My lifeline

and my soul mate.

The Cliff Birds

✣

A Story of Hope

Far away from here lies an island you won't find on any map. It is a place of beauty and color, unspoiled by the presence of man. The island thrusts up out of the sea like the arm of a giant reaching for the stars. The air is rich with sound: surf crashing against rugged cliffs, the splash of many waterfalls, and the lovely calls of birds of every description and type.

But if you had gone there many years ago, no matter how hard you might have listened, you would not have heard the rustle of wings in the air, nor would you have seen birds in flight. For flight passed away from this land so many years ago that none of the birds there even remembered that it was possible.

Instead, they contented themselves with walking about on the ground or just hopping along. They all had come to believe that attempting to fly would mean sure death.

No one knows how the island birds came to have such a mistaken idea, for nothing is more natural than that birds should fly. Nevertheless, somewhere far back in the dim mists of time, these birds had come to believe something that wasn't true, and as a result their lives had grown extremely limited and dull.

On that faraway island lived Sweenie, a solid-blue parrot. Any scientist who had ever seen Sweenie would have exclaimed, "Ah! A hyacinth macaw!" But to himself Sweenie was — well, just Sweenie.

Strangely, just as he was coming into the prime of his parrothood, Sweenie had become extremely unhappy. *There has to be more to a bird's life than this,* he often thought. *Life here is so dull and meaningless! I can't explain it, but I just have a feeling that I am missing out on something great.*

Sweenie glanced about Skerry, the small portion of the island where the birds lived. He himself had never left Skerry and knew of only two birds who had dared to go beyond its borders. Both trips had ended badly. One of the two adventurers, Sweenie's grandfather Adelar, had left and never returned. The other, his Aunt Tambee, had returned, but with a broken wing. So of course the idea of venturing beyond his known world made Sweenie afraid.

And yet he was constantly plagued by the notion that the remedy for his feeling of emptiness had to do with flying, and that the answer was out there somewhere — beyond the limits of Skerry.

From time to time Sweenie mentioned his feeling to his Aunt Tambee. She nodded wisely, just listening and watching to see how Sweenie would handle his inner unrest. She felt sure she would know what to say when the time for speaking came.

Each afternoon the birds of Skerry gathered to listen to stories of excitement and terror. Of all the birds, only a few were honored by election to the position of storyteller. It was every young bird's dream.

One particular afternoon a sulfur-crested cockatoo named Maelle had the privilege of telling the tales. Her story was a familiar favorite, a sure-fire crowd-pleaser — a recital of the terrible things that happen to birds who attempt to fly.

Maelle had the full attention of her audience as she finished her tale. "We all suspect what happened to Adelar. And we have all heard stories of how Tambee broke that wing of hers. But today you have heard the real reason. It was simply that Tambee tried to fly, and as we know only too well, she was lucky that all she suffered was a broken wing."

As Sweenie perched outside his home tree listening to Maelle's story, at first he felt surprised and shocked. And then he began to feel angry. The longer he listened, the angrier he became. *I can't believe Maelle is saying these things about my Aunt Tambee,* he thought. *Everyone is soaking up every word, like she's telling the truth set in stone! My Aunt Tambee isn't the*

fool that Maelle pictures her to be. Surely she would never climb
up into the cliffs and try to fly back down!

Next day Sweenie still felt angry about the story. He
brought it up with his best friend, a cockatiel called Wylie. "You
know, Wylie, I didn't like that story Maelle told about my Aunt

Tambee yesterday. It isn't right to tell stories that are untrue —
especially when someone's reputation is at stake."

Sweenie's friend had a ready answer. "Calm down, pal. Since
when did actual facts have anything to do with a story? A story
isn't half as good if it only tells the facts." Wylie flipped upside

down on his perch. "For goodness' sake, Sweenie, a storyteller stretching the truth is nothing new."

But Sweenie would not be pacified. "This isn't just any old story," he shouted. "Maelle is dragging down my Aunt Tambee, and everybody believes her, even though no one else has any finer character than my Aunt Tambee!"

"Whoa there, partner, not so loud," cautioned Wylie.

"I don't care if they hear me," Sweenie cried. "And you want to know something else? I've been thinking it over, and I'm beginning to believe there's no reason why we have to be so afraid of flying. So there!"

"Hey, that's crazy talk, Sweenie. You better watch yourself. Here's a quick reality check, cockatiel to macaw," Wylie said. "It's against the law of Skerry even to discuss flight as a serious possibility. You know if they catch you trying it, it's over the cliffs for you. You either wind up dying trying flying, or dying for trying flying. Get it?" Wylie finished with a grin.

"Yeah, yeah, I get it, you goose." Sweenie grinned in spite of himself. "It's hard to stay angry with a clown like you around."

For the rest of that day Sweenie mulled over everything he had heard and the thoughts he was having about flying. He remembered an important lesson his Aunt Tambee had taught him — that it's always best to discuss upsetting situations with trusted friends. "Your secrets will eventually make you sick," Tambee had said. "Be completely honest about what upsets you. Don't keep any part of it to yourself."

By bedtime Sweenie felt a tiny bit better after telling Wylie his feelings and thoughts, but when he awakened the next morning with the same old subject still bothering him, he hopped over to Aunt Tambee's home to get her point of view.

"I'm glad to see you, Sweenie." Tambee's voice was gentle and kind. "Perch right here next to me."

"I'm glad to see you, too," said Sweenie as he settled down. "You know you told me always to discuss anything that upsets me with someone I trust. Well, I'm upset now, and I trust you, so I came to talk about it."

"That's good," she said. "I suspect you're looking for a remedy for a hurtful situation. Is that right?"

"Exactly," said Sweenie. "I'm angry about some of the things people are saying about you, and I want to make them stop."

"I see," said Tambee, cocking her head on one side and looking thoughtful and wise. "You want to stop other birds saying bad things about me. Well, Sweenie dear, the fact is that no matter how hard you try, you cannot control the behavior of other birds."

"Maybe not, but I can fight fire with fire. I'll teach them a lesson, give them a dose of their own medicine! I'll tell some lies about them!"

"Oh, my, Sweenie, now you're talking about revenge, and there are two problems with that. The first is that going out for revenge only leaves you feeling worse, not better. The second is that you don't fix the problem — you only make it bigger."

"Well, at least I can hate them, can't I?"

"Of course you can," said Aunt Tambee, "if you want to punish yourself." She spread her good wing around Sweenie. "Tell me — after you have hated and felt angry for a while, how does that feel to you?"

"To tell the truth, it doesn't feel good," said Sweenie. "When I let myself stay filled with hate and anger, I lose my appetite. I have trouble sleeping. I get in a bad mood, too, so that no one likes to have me around."

"There!" Tambee nodded. "Thank you for being so honest. Really, Sweenie, the only control any of us has in scary situations is deciding how to respond. Others may lie about us, or about someone we care for. They may also turn against us and turn others against us. They may do hurtful things. And we can't stop them. Such things do happen."

"The important thing to remember is that you will always have a choice as to how to behave in response. *You* can choose how *you* will respond. Such situations turn tragic only if the one who has been hurt becomes like all the others, answering their lies with more lies, hating them, nursing anger, trying to settle the score."

"Do you know what your grandfather Adelar told me on the last morning before he disappeared? 'Tambee,' he said, 'you must decide which side to be on. My advice is, stick with the truth. Because if you don't, dishonesty, anger, and hate will eventually make you crazy.' And of course he was right."

Sweenie chimed in, knowing parts of the story well. "And after that he set out for the cliffs, hoping to follow the waterfalls to the top. Aunt Tambee, you never told me what he hoped to find up there. What was it? Did he find it?"

Tambee had a sad, faraway look in her eyes, as if she were watching her father leave Skerry all over again. "He was seeking the answer to the same question you've been asking lately," she said.

"You mean my grandfather felt lost and incomplete, the same as I feel?"

"That's right," said Tambee. "I tried to stop him. I begged him to stay. 'What if you are killed?' I cried after him as he left. He paused, turned to look back, shook his head, and said, 'Sometimes it's enough just to take the first steps, even when the remaining steps have to be taken by someone else.' You know the rest. I went after him the next day, but I never knew if he found what he was looking for. The only thing I have to show for it is this broken wing."

Long after their talk was over, Tambee's words stayed with Sweenie.

A few nights later, Sweenie had a dream in which he himself followed the waterfalls to the cliff tops. And when he reached his goal, he was astonished to see standing before him a fearsome raptor, a bird of prey. Even though the Skerry storytellers loved to describe the great predatory birds, Sweenie had never imagined any bird existed that was so enormous or so powerful. Somehow he knew that the bird of his dream must be an eagle.

In Sweenie's dream, the eagle took Sweenie up in his huge wings, and from that moment Sweenie no longer felt afraid. As the great bird lifted Sweenie from his perch on the rocks, their eyes locked together, and Sweenie was overcome by the deep love and compassion shining forth from the eagle's eyes.

Amazing, thought Sweenie. *So huge, so strong, yet unable to hate anyone!*

"Sweenie," the eagle said, "follow your heart and become what you were meant to be — what you already are. If you go deep within yourself you will find the strength there to overcome the fear that has always stood in your way." And that was the end of the dream.

Before the sun rose in the morning Sweenie awoke knowing what he had to do. Taking nothing with him but his courage, he set out on his journey toward the waterfalls, still in the darkness. *It's really true what they say,* he thought as he shivered in the chilly air. *It* is *always darkest and coldest just before dawn.*

The first light of morning was breaking over the far horizon by the time Sweenie reached the stream. He took one last look at the ocean, then turned and started upward along the flowing water's side, walking at times, at other times hopping from rock to rock. Everything he saw was unfamiliar, and he found the new sights beautiful and exciting. As he came to one waterfall after another, each one seemed quite wonderful in its own way.

Soon Sweenie was feeling disgusted with himself for having waited so long to discover all this magnificence. *I could have been enjoying all of this long before now,* he told himself, *if I hadn't been afraid to venture outside Skerry.*

He forged determinedly ahead for hours as the way grew steeper. By afternoon the young macaw had become quite hungry and extremely tired. Just as he was wondering what in the world he would do for food, he came to a ledge beside the next waterfall where a strange creature was cracking nuts with a rock.

"What's the matter?" the creature asked as Sweenie stared. "Haven't you ever seen a monkey before?"

No, Sweenie had never seen a monkey. If this was a monkey, it certainly had a warm and friendly face. The monkey smiled. "Please — help yourself to these nuts. You look starved."

Sweenie *was* starved. He decided to trust this odd creature, hopping up and sampling a nut, then hungrily snatching up a whole beakful. "Delicious!" he exclaimed. "I've never seen such

nuts as these. Where did they come from? Can you show me? I don't want to be a nuisance, but could I — "

"For one so hungry, you ask a lot of questions," said the friendly monkey. "You eat. I'll talk."

The monkey set aside his nutcracker stone and looked at Sweenie intently. "Let's see what I can figure out. You're traveling upstream — that's obvious. Your intended destination must be — the cliff tops."

Sweenie nodded.

"Okay," said the monkey, pleased with himself. "You're searching for something — yes — you've set out on a quest!"

"I'm impressed," Sweenie mumbled, his beak full of cracked nuts. "Yes, I have set out on a quest. I need to know whether we birds can fly."

"Is that all? It's simple! See that tree there? Climb it and jump."

"No, it's not simple," said the doubtful bird. "I'm sure there's a lot of stuff you have to do first. You know, preparations, demonstrations, instructions, all such as that."

"If you say so," the monkey replied. "By the way, what's your name?"

"Sweenie. And yours?"

"I'm Malachi. Pleased to meet you, Sweenie. Well, Sweenie, think about this. I suspect that what you are up to is bigger than you think. It's not just about being able to fly. It's also about changing sides."

"Huh?" Now Sweenie was thoroughly confused. Hadn't he heard those same words from someone else before?

"Changing sides is about waking up to all of reality — what you can see and the part that you can't see," Malachi went on. "It's about becoming part of the solution and no longer part of the problem."

"You lost me there somewhere," Sweenie said.

Malachi chuckled. "Don't worry. It will make more sense with time. Right now you just need to know one important thing, which is that it gets freezing cold on the cliff tops after dark. Whatever you do, don't let nightfall catch you still there. The wind gets rough up there most evenings, too, with vicious downdrafts. It's probably going to take you two, maybe three days to walk that far. But don't lose your courage, and don't give up hope. *I believe you can do it.*"

The first part of Malachi's report left Sweenie feeling discouraged, so much so that he found it hard to take in Malachi's very important final words. However, with much encouragement from Malachi and many more nuts, Sweenie eventually reclaimed his will to go on. At last the macaw and the monkey bid each other farewell, and Sweenie set out to continue his quest.

"Oh, one last thing, Sweenie," Malachi called after him. "A waterfall upstream drops over a big cave. It's a good place to spend the night. You can't miss it."

"Thank you from the bottom of my heart," Sweenie shouted back. Then with a sigh he continued on.

Sure enough, Sweenie found the cave under the waterfall and settled in for a comfortable sleep. But as the full darkness of night enveloped him, his imagination gave life to every tiny noise, so that cold fear took over again. *Oh, why did I think I could make this trip?* he moaned. A clattering noise echoing around the cave walls really scared him, until Sweenie realized it was his own beak vibrating with fear.

Suddenly, quite close by, a voice boomed out of the darkness. "What in confounded consternation is that rattling racket?"

Sweenie squawked, nearly fainting with fright.

"Oh, it's only a bird," the darkness spoke reassuringly. "Where are my manners? Let me get the lights — okay, boys, your time to shine."

Sweenie heard paws clapping together several times, followed by sudden illumination of the cave. The soft green glow of several dozen fireflies clumped together on a leaf lighted up a black-and-grey raccoon sitting in a corner.

"How do you like my invention?" the raccoon said. "I call it the light bug." He laughed. "So — you're a parrot. I knew you were coming. Just didn't know what you would be. Oh, by the way — " the raccoon gestured with his thumb at his own face — "don't let this mask worry you. I'm as harmless as a hickory nut. My name's Shandey. Who are you?"

"Sweenie," the parrot stammered. "You remind me of a cockatiel friend of mine."

"Is that so!" The raccoon struck a debonair pose. "He must be a handsome fellow, then." Shandey slapped his knee jovially and laughed again. "So, Sweenie, what can I do for you?"

"Well, I'm curious. You said you knew I was coming. How?"

"Oh, I just knew. Maybe a quick story will make you understand."

"I love a story if it's a good one," said Sweenie. "Do tell."

Shandey cleared his throat to begin. "I was stranded just downstream in that very river, on a rock smack-dab at the top of the highest fall. Far up on the cliff tops a hard downpour had fallen, and the stream was rising by the minute, with water simply roaring down. I was sure I was about to be washed down the waterfall to die.

"In the nick of time I happened to notice a tree limb hanging over the fall, and an uncharacteristic thought struck me — *Jump for it!* Well, we raccoons are rotten jumpers, and

I had no doubt that that branch was well out of my range. Still the waters rose.

"The same thought repeated itself several times — *Jump for it! Jump for it!* — exactly as if another voice was talking inside my head. Let me tell you, I was scared stiff! The water was already up to my neck when that same something inside my head urged me, *Go ahead — jump! You can make it!*"

Listening breathlessly, Sweenie croaked, "What happened?"

Shandey solemnly bowed his head. "Well — I drowned." Then with a chuckle he got back to the facts. "No, of course I didn't drown. I just jumped, for Pete's sake! But here's where it gets weird. I knew I wasn't going to make it. And then something grabbed me in mid-air and carried me far enough to reach out and catch that branch. And as you see, here I am today."

Sweenie's beak fell open. "That's a wonderful story! But what was it that saved you?"

"I never got a glimpse of it, even though I looked in all directions as I clung to that limb. Regardless of what it may have been, that day marked the beginning of an amazing change for me. Now I often have these odd thoughts that don't seem natural to me, as if I'm being told to do something I ordinarily might not do, or as if I know something I ordinarily wouldn't know. And if it seems I'm being told to do a thing, even something I've been afraid to do, now I follow the thought and go ahead to do it. And amazing things happen as a result.

"Here's why I'm telling you my story — one of those odd thoughts told me someone was coming who would need my help. And someone did come. The someone was you."

Sweenie rocked onto his back claws, astonished by Shandey's tale. The two of them went on talking far into the night with Sweenie feeling more and more reassured until finally he fell into a deep, restful sleep.

Next morning when Sweenie awoke Shandey was gone, but he had left a good amount of nuts and two apples for the parrot. *Thanks, good friend,* thought Sweenie as he ate his

fill, gathering strength for the day. And then with his
stomach full and his mind restored Sweenie resumed his
journey upstream.

The second day of travel took a heavy toll on the young
parrot, and by the middle of the afternoon he was exhausted.

I'll just rest my aching feet a few minutes, he thought
as he stretched out on a flat rock near a stream.

The next thing he knew, he was awakened by warm
breath on his face. Sweenie lay perfectly still, not daring to
open his eyes.

"Pardon me, but are you dead perhaps?" a gentle voice inquired. "That would be a pity. I would have offered you a ride if you were going my way."

Sweenie cracked open one eye. "I'm headed for the cliff tops. If you're traveling upstream, I'd love a ride."

"Climb up between my shoulders and get comfortable," said the animal. "I'm a bighorn sheep, name of Trahern. Get some rest, and I'll let you know when we arrive."

Trying to roost on something that was moving rapidly made sleep impossible for Sweenie. But he was very grateful, because the way up the cliffs became so difficult that he knew he could never have made it on his own. By the end of the afternoon Trahern halted and announced, "This is as far as I can go. The top of the island is straight up there."

Despairing, Sweenie stared at the sheer cliff wall. "I can't make it," he whispered.

"Climb onto my horn," Trahern directed calmly. "I'll toss you up. Now don't worry. I'm a terrific tosser, and I have a very strong neck."

"It's not the throw that scares me, it's the landing."

"Never you mind," Trahern reassured the bird. "And listen, Sweenie, when you get up there, I want you to remember something. You are never alone, not ever. The strength you need is right there with you. Just ask for it, then do what you have to do." Trahern lowered his head toward the ground. "Now brace yourself," he said.

"N-no, wait!" Sweenie tried to say. But it was too late. With the cliff behind him, the bighorn flipped his head up and then back, launching Sweenie like a badminton birdie over the top of the great rock wall.

Afterward Trahern held his breath until he spied Sweenie peering down over the cliff edge at him.

"Hey! That wasn't so bad," Sweenie yelled. "Thanks! I can't tell you how much help you've been."

"My pleasure," said Trahern. "Take care until we meet again." The surefooted sheep turned and picked his way back down the rocks as Sweenie watched from above.

A strong cool wind was blowing as Sweenie settled down to look around him and think about exploring the cliff tops. His excitement at having reached his goal soon gave way to concern. *There's no one here to answer my questions,* he worried, *no one to show me how it's done.* He gazed up at the clouds swirling above him. Had he come all this way for nothing?

Suddenly the clouds parted, and a single sunbeam focused on a nearby rock. There was no mistaking it. The rock was shaped like — a bird in flight! Sweenie hurriedly hopped over to the rock so he could study it closely. The ray of light dimmed and vanished. Sweenie peered gingerly over the cliff's edge. Above and around him were only gray clouds, below him a thick, bottomless mist.

"Is this all I get?" he shouted into the curtain of clouds.

And at that moment a quiet, calm voice like an uncharacteristic thought spoke inside Sweenie's head: *Fly.*

Sweenie stepped to the edge and gazed down. The wind had strengthened, whipping the mist below into a seething blur. He sank back. "I can't do it," he said out loud.

The voice came again, more insistent this time: FLY!

"I need someone to show me how!" Sweenie shrieked. "Before I jump off this cliff, I'll sit up here and freeze to death!"

Some of us have weeks, some of us have months to make decisions that will forever change our lives. Sweenie's decision

came in a few quick seconds. A sudden roar surrounded him, like thunder coming from everywhere at once. Was it a storm cloud? Sweenie turned his head to confront, not a storm cloud, but a cougar crouching atop a log, fangs bared, gazing hungrily at him.

Sweenie's fear paralyzed him. A rumble came from deep in the cougar's throat, as though something terrible was trapped there, trying to get out. The big cat's eyes blazed as a second roar exploded through his awful fangs. He sprang over the log toward Sweenie, rapidly closing the distance between.

FLY!! sang the thought in Sweenie's head. YOU CAN DO IT!!

"Please help me!" Sweenie prayed in terror, and then he jumped.

The cougar never hesitated, leaping over the edge after the bird. Immediately, violent downdraft winds tossed Sweenie about. He beat his wings furiously, trying to gain control. As the cougar fell toward the desperate bird, suddenly the big cat seemed to vanish, and a great eagle appeared in its place.

Above Sweenie the eagle spread his huge wings into the mist, completely blocking the fierce winds. Sweenie never knew quite how it happened, but the downdrafts from the cliffs released him so that he was able to gain control of his wings, however unsteady they seemed. Dread turned to elation. Sweenie was FLYING!

And thus they continued flying, parrot and guardian eagle, down the cliffs and beyond, until they reached the calm skies over Skerry.

In Skerry itself the situation was anything but calm. By nightfall of the first day of Sweenie's disappearance search parties had been organized. Wylie recounted the last conversation he had had with Sweenie, and among the birds suspicion and rumor began to point to Tambee. By the second evening a nearly hysterical mob of birds converged on her home.

A storyteller was the first to accuse her. "Tambee, all your crazy talk about self-improvement, chasing your dreams, all that nonsense — that's exactly what put ideas in that youngster's head!"

"We're certain Sweenie has come to a cruel end — no doubt trying to fly!" another added. "No question about it. Tambee, you're a danger to all of Skerry's young impressionable minds."

Aldric, the revered chief storyteller, solemnly raised his wings to silence the crowd. "Tambee," he said, "several

years ago, when you hurt your wing, we could never prove that you attempted to fly. Today it's clear that we should have worked harder to prove what a wrong thing you had done.

"Now you're encouraging others to break one of the very laws that are the glue of our society. Not a one of us is safe with such a rebel as you lurking in our midst!"

"I say we push her over the cliff!" someone shouted. "Death to Tambee — over the cliff!"

"Over the cliff!" rose up a chorus from the mob. As they chanted, the birds surged forward, forcing Tambee to the very edge.

But Sweenie's aunt was a very brave parrot. "First, hear me out!" she cried. "Then, by crackers, do your worst!"

The crowd fell silent.

"Why does change frighten all of you so? Are you so content with this dull way of life that you would kill to protect it?"

She searched their faces. "Open your minds for just one moment! See if you can imagine how wonderful and thrilling it would be to actually fly! Swooping and darting among the clouds, with the wind whistling through your feathers, without a care in the world — why, it's beyond our wildest dreams! Freedom, with no fear of falling! A wonderful freedom like nothing any of us has ever known!"

"What if there were only one chance in a million that every bird among you could actually fly? Wouldn't you just have to take that chance? Of course you would!"

"Enough of this rubbish!" Aldric broke in. "You're a sly one, Tambee, a slick one, but your time has run out!"

"No!" shouted a green parrot. "Wait! She just might have a point."

"I stand with Tambee too!" yelled a cockatoo. "I need to know whether flight is possible!"

"Yes, I agree! We should go to any length necessary to find out!" chimed in a scarlet macaw.

Another awesome moment of silence fell as everyone considered this revolutionary thought. And in that silence a strange sound was heard overhead, growing louder by the second — the sound of wings surging through the air.

Looking up, the birds were amazed to see a hyacinth macaw fly straight toward them, then dart up to perch in a

tree. Could it be — was it — yes, it was! Sweenie made a sweeping circle above the group, then settled nonchalantly onto a rock. "Hey, Aldric, what's up?"

Several weeks later, Sweenie and Tambee stood together quietly gazing at the horizon far out to sea.

"You know, Sweenie, lately I've noticed something very different about you," his aunt said. "I've seen a change that seems to go deeper than just having become the hero of Skerry."

Sweenie cocked his head with a quizzical look.

"Up there in the cliffs I think you must have discovered something bigger than flight."

Sweenie nodded. "You're right. Aunt Tambee, I'm awake now, like you. My eyes have been opened, and I've started on a new quest."

"What's that? Is there something more important than flying?"

"Oh, yes. Something very important indeed. It's funny how I thought flying was the thing that would fill me up inside. Flying has been my dream. And now that I can do it, it does make me happy.

"But it's the thing that made it possible for me to realize my dream that's truly made me whole. Up there on the cliffs, I met something wonderful, something great and peaceful and loving, something larger and more powerful than anything else I have ever known. I don't know its name, and I can't fully describe it, but I'm a part of it now, and it's a part of me."

Tambee smiled. "You've changed sides, haven't you?"

"Definitely," said Sweenie. "Now I'm on a different journey. It's so wonderful! I just want to go deeper into it, to know it better."

Tambee beamed at
the brave young bird.
"How fine! Sweenie dear,
I want you to know that
I will help you all I can."

She turned to peer
at a cockatoo in flight.
"Oh, my, is that who I
think it is?"

"I don't believe it!"
Sweenie cheered. "Aldric
has taken up flying!"

Tambee and Sweenie
wrapped their wings
around each other in a
big hug, then laughed
out loud for the sheer joy
of life. And from that
day to this, not a single
bird in Skerry has been
afraid to fly. ❧

Acknowledgments

For technical and material support, deep gratitude to Kristi and Welbert Deese, Rob Russo, Lynn Howard, Jim Fauber, Jon Rasula, and Derrick Davis.

For spiritual support above and beyond the call, all my dear friends at the RPC, especially Tammy Bell, Mike Weeks, Jim Phillips, and Doug Robertson.

Appreciation to everyone at the WFHG, particularly Gary Thrailkill, Tony Daddona, and KC Jones, and everyone at the MCCSG, especially Amy and Gary Christian and Linda Essick.

Thanks to Toby Rice Drews, Recovery Communications, Inc., and editor Betsy Tice White for the opportunity of letting Sweenie tell his tale.

For 15 years **Miles A. Moody** was a small-animal veterinarian. Having worked through deep emotional pain in his life and thereby finding a much happier way of being, he resolved to use story-telling and art to contribute to the healing of others. Living in North Carolina with his wife Lynne and two young children, Miles welcomes any opportunity to share his message of recovery, inspiration and hope.

Additional copies of this book
are available from the author.

To order, copy and fill in this order blank
and mail it with your check.
(Please print all information clearly.)

Name: _____

Address: _____

City: _____ State: _____ Zip: _____

Phone: _____

_____ Copies @ $19.95 per copy = $ _____

NC residents add 6% sales tax   _____

Add for shipping & handling $ $3.50

TOTAL $ _____

**Mail order with
check payable to Miles A. Moody to:
273 Fryling Avenue S.W.
Concord, NC 28025**

Recovery Communications, Inc.

BOOK PUBLISHING & AUTHOR PROMOTIONS
Post Office Box 19910 • Baltimore, Maryland 21211, USA

Now available through your local bookstore!

Jennifer J. Richardson, M.S.W. *Diary of Abuse/Diary of Healing.* A young girl's secret journal recording two decades of abuse, with detailed healing therapy sessions. A raw and extraordinary book that will inspire other abuse survivors with new hope. **Contact the author at (404) 373-1837.**

Toby Rice Drews. *Getting Them Sober, Volume One — You Can Help!* Hundreds of ideas for sobriety and recovery. The million-seller endorsed by Melody Beattie, Dr. Norman Vincent Peale, and "Dear Abby." **Contact the author at (410) 243-8352.**

Toby Rice Drews. *Getting Them Sober, Volume Four — Separation Decisions.* All about detachment, separation, and child custody issues for families of alcoholics. A "book of immense value," says Max Weisman, M.D., past president of the American Society of Addiction Medicine. **Contact the author at (410) 243-8352.**

Betsy Tice White. *Turning Your Teen Around: How A Couple Helped Their Troubled Son While Keeping Their Marriage Alive and Well.* A doctor family's successful personal battle against teen-age drug use, with powerfully helpful tips for parents in pain. Endorsed by John Palmer, former news anchor, NBC's TODAY Show. **Contact the author at (770) 590-7311.**

Betsy Tice White. *Mountain Folk/Mountain Food: Down-Home Wisdom, Plain Tales, and Recipe Secrets from Appalachia.* The joy of living as expressed in delightful vignettes and mouth-watering regional foods. Endorsed by the Discovery Channel's "Great Country Inns" and *Blue Ridge Country Magazine.* **Contact the author at (770) 590-7311.**

(more on next page)

Linda Meyer, Ph.D. *I See Myself Changing: Weekly Meditations and Recovery Journaling for Young Adults.* A life-affirming book for adolescents and young adults, endorsed by Robert Bulkeley of The Gilman School. **Contact the author at (217) 367-8821.**

Linda Meyer, Ph.D. *Why Is It So Hard To Take Care Of My Parent?* The only book that deals head-on with the nitty-gritty of eldercare issues in dysfunctional families. **Contact the author at (217) 367-8821.**

Mattie Carroll Mullins. *JUDY: The Murder of My Daughter, The Healing of My Family.* A Christian mother's inspiring story of how her family moved from unimaginable tragedy to forgiveness. **Contact the author at (423) 926-7827.**

Mattie Carroll Mullins. *Preachers' Wives Tell All! Lively Tales and Tasty Recipes from Country Parsonage Kitchens.* The lighter side of life from the point of view of the pastor's helpmate, with plenty of appetizing recipes thrown in. **Contact the author at (423) 926-7827.**

Joseph C. Buccilli, Ph.D. *Wise Stuff About Relationships: Spiritual Reflections and Recovery Journal.* A gem of a book for anyone in recovery; "an empowering spiritual workout." Endorsed by the vice-president of the *Philadelphia Inquirer.* **Contact the author at (609) 629-4441.**

Stacie Hagan and Charlie Palmgren. *The Chicken Conspiracy: Breaking the Cycle of Personal Stress and Organizational Mediocrity.* A liberating message from corporate trainers about successful personal, organizational, and global change. **Contact the authors at (404) 297-9388.**

David E. Bergesen. *Murder Crosses the Equator: A Father Jack Carthier Mystery.* Volcanic tale of suspense in a Latin-American setting, starring a clever missionary-priest detective. **Contact the author at (520) 744-2631.**

John Pearson. *Eastern Shore Beckonings.* Marvelous trek back in time through charming villages and encounters with solid Chesapeake Bay folk. "Aches with affection" — The *Village Voice's* Washington correspondent. **Contact the author at (410) 315-7940.**

Jerry Zeller. *The Shaman and Other Almost-Tall Tales.* The enchantment of story-telling and grace-filled character sketches from an Episcopal archdeacon and former Emory University Dean. **Contact the author at (706) 692-5842.**

Jane Griz Jones. *From Grief to Gladness: Coming Back From Widowhood.* A Christian educator shares personal heartbreak and wisdom for reclaiming joy in life. **Contact the author at (706) 216-4559.**